Whale Summer

Whale Summer

Penn Mullin
AR B.L.: 3.0
Points: 1.0

UG

Cover Design Illustrations: Tina Cash

International Standard Book Number: 0-87879-910-9

09 08 97 96 05 04 03 02
9 8 7 6 5 4

You'll enjoy all the High Noon Books. Write for
a free full list of titles.

Contents

CHAPTER 1

Summer Job

Mark and Jason sat down at the back of the bus.

"Gosh, it's hot in here. When are we going to get our own wheels?" Jason said. He pushed open the bus window. A warm breeze came through the window.

"As soon as we save up some money. That's when," Mark answered. "And we have to think about gas, too. Having a car is going to be pretty expensive I think. We can only afford a used car so we will probably need extra money for repairs now and then."

"Only two weeks till school's out. We better get some jobs set up," Jason said.

"Got any ideas?" Mark asked.

"No. I checked on those lifeguard jobs. They're all taken," Jason said. "People sign up for them in the winter."

"We could try working at Ed's again," Mark said. "Maybe he would even give us a little more money. We did a pretty good job for him last year. We didn't miss a single day."

"No way. Last summer was enough. I don't want to pump gas again for a long time," said Jason. "Unless it's for our own car. I want to do something exciting this summer. Something new and different."

"What—like test-driving race cars?" Mark laughed.

"OK. OK. I know you think we don't have a chance for any neat jobs." Jason looked out the window. "Hey! I just thought of something." He pointed to a large sign. It showed a picture of a huge black and white whale. "Sea Center! Maybe we could get jobs there! What a great way to spend a summer!"

"Sure. They'll let us train the killer whales. Come on. Here's our stop." Mark started for the door of the bus. Jason followed.

"But it's worth a try, Mark. It's a great place. Remember that show we saw last summer? The whales did all those great tricks? Maybe we could work in one of the shows," Jason said. "Just think what it would be like to be right down there beside the whale tank."

The boys got off the bus and started walking home.

"I'm sure that all the jobs are probably gone by now," Mark said.

"Let's stop by Sea Center tomorrow after school. We can check it out, OK?" Jason asked. "Anyway, all they can say is no. And just maybe we'll be lucky."

"OK. We'll give it a try." Mark and Jason touched hands in the high five sign. "But don't get your hopes up. There must be hundreds of high school kids out looking for summer jobs right now."

Jason smiled at Mark. He knew his brother was probably right. But a summer at Sea Center would sure beat pumping gas at Ed's!

CHAPTER 2

Sea Center

The next day Mark and Jason took the bus to Sea Center. They asked at the front gate where to find out about jobs.

"Carla Brown is the person to see. Go to the second building on your right," the guard told the boys.

Mark and Jason walked into Sea Center. There were big crowds of people there. Everyone seemed excited. Loudspeakers told about times for the next whale show.

Jason's stomach felt all tight inside. Maybe it was stupid to even ask. But you can't lose anything by trying.

The boys went into the building that the

guard told them about.

"Hi. I'm Sara. May I help you?" A pretty girl was sitting at a desk inside.

"Yes, we're here to ask about summer

Mark and Jason walked into Sea Center.

jobs," Mark said.

"OK. First you need to fill out these forms. Then you can go in to see Carla Brown." Sara gave Mark and Jason some papers and pens.

"You can sit over there," she said.

The boys sat at a table. They had to write down their names, ages, and where they lived. Then there was a space for writing what other jobs they'd had.

"I wrote down our job at Ed's. Should we tell about our lawnmowing job, too?" Jason asked Mark.

"Sure. That was a job. And our paper route," Mark said. "The more jobs we've had the better we look!"

The boys finished writing. Then they gave the forms to Sara.

"Please wait while I take these to Carla," she said. "She will want to take a minute to look them over before she talks to you."

Soon Sara took Mark and Jason into Carla

Brown's office. Carla was a tall, friendly-looking woman.

"I'm Carla Brown." She shook hands with Mark and Jason. "You must be Mark. You're one year older, right?" Carla asked Mark.

"Yes. We're a year apart," Mark said.

"And you've always had summer jobs together. I read that on the forms you wrote," Carla said. "I hope we can find you jobs here at Sea Center. Have a seat, boys."

The boys sat down on a couch by Carla's desk. Jason started to relax a little. Maybe there are some jobs left! Maybe even something in the whale show!

"Well, most of our summer jobs are already taken," Carla said. "I'll tell you what's left." She looked at some papers on her desk. "We still need help at the main snack bar. And one ticket seller job is left. Would either of those jobs interest you fellows?"

"Aren't there any jobs in the whale show?"

Jason asked. She probably would think he was crazy to ask this. Everybody would want those jobs first.

"Well, how are you at handling fish?" Carla asked with a smile.

"You mean the whales?" Jason sat up straighter.

"No, sorry. Our trainers do that," Carla said. "We need helpers to fill buckets of fish. The trainers give the whales fish as rewards for tricks."

"Would we do other things, too—besides the fish?" Mark asked.

"Yes. You'd help keep people in their seats. Away from the pool. The trainers will keep you busy. That's for sure," Carla said. She smiled at the boys.

"Sounds great to me! I never thought we could be in the whale show," Jason said. He looked at Mark. Would Mark go for it or did the fish buckets turn him off?

"How much would the job pay?" Mark asked Carla.

"Five dollars an hour. If you stay all summer you get a bonus. You get two days off a week," Carla said.

Five an hour. That was more than Ed paid when they'd worked at the gas station. And there was a bonus if you stayed all summer. I'll take the whale show over pumping gas any day, Jason thought. But what about Mark? Would he agree?

"Carla, could Mark and I go outside and talk for a minute?" Jason asked.

"Sure. Go ahead. I'll be here for another half hour," Carla said.

The boys went outside to talk.

"Filling fish buckets! We'd smell like fish all summer. I can just hear what the guys would say," Mark said. "No way. They'd have to pay me more than five an hour and give me more days off, too!"

"Mark, it wouldn't be so bad. We'd be part of the whale show. The fish bucket stuff is only a small part of the job. And the pay is OK. We'll have wheels by the end of summer. Don't forget that bonus," Jason said. "That could be pretty nice."

"Yeah, the pay is OK. But fish buckets! Maybe I should work in the snack bar instead," Mark said. "You could still do the whale show."

"But we've always worked together. Let's give it a try. Then you can change if you really hate it." Jason put his arm on his brother's shoulder. "Trust me, Mark."

"Well, I'll give it a couple of weeks. We might as well both smell like fish, I guess. How did I let you talk me into this?" Mark laughed and gave Jason the high five.

"Hey, great, Mark! I bet it's going to be super," Jason said.

" Well, Jason, do you think any girls will

11

come near us this summer?" Mark laughed.

"Maybe not. But I bet they'll like the car we'll be driving next fall!" Jason answered. "Let's go tell Carla we'll take the job!"

CHAPTER 3

First Day

The days went by slowly till school got out. Jason couldn't wait to start at Sea Center. Mark wasn't so excited. He tried not to think about it. He wasn't so sure any more that he should have let Jason talk him into the job. I'll give it a fair chance, he thought, maybe for a week or two.

Starting day finally came. Mrs. Conway dropped Mark and Jason off at Sea Center on her way to work.

"Don't have fish for dinner tonight, Mom!" Mark laughed as they got out of the car. "I have a feeling that I may never want to look at a fish again after today."

"Good luck, boys!" Mrs. Conway waved and drove off.

"Let's go get our uniforms," Jason said. They went into the men's locker room.

Other guys were getting dressed for work. Mark found two blue jumpsuits hanging on a rack.

"These two have our names on them. Let's do it." The boys started getting into the uniforms.

A thin dark-haired boy came over to them. "Hi, I'm Pete Brooks. This your first day at Sea Center?"

"Yep, first day. I'm Mark Conway and this is my brother Jason. You new here, too?" Mark asked.

"No. I was here last summer. What have they got you guys doing?"

"Whale show," Jason said.

"Hey, that'll keep you busy. I did it last summer. It's hard to make people stay in their seats. And I hope you like the smell of fish!" Pete laughed.

Mark gave Jason an "I told you so" look.

"What job do you have this summer?" Mark asked.

"Snack bar. I'm not super at making snowcones. But I sure get to meet great-looking girls!" Pete waved as he went out the door. "See you later!"

"Hey, Mark, cheer up. Maybe a beautiful girl will fall into the whale pool. Then you can rescue her," Jason laughed as he zipped up his jumpsuit.

"Fat chance," Mark said. "Well, I guess we should go out to the whale pool. That's where they told us to meet the trainer."

The boys started out of the locker room. Some of the guys smiled and waved to them. Everybody seemed really friendly. Jason had a good feeling about the place. He hoped Mark would, too. They walked out into the bright

15

sunshine and looked around.

"Gosh, this is a big place!" Jason said.

They looked up at all the seats around the whale pool. The rows went very high. There seemed to be hundreds of seats.

"Are you two Mark and Jason?" A tall girl in a white jumpsuit waved. She was sitting beside the whale pool. There was a set of small bottles next to her.

The boys walked over to her.

"Welcome to Sea Center. I'm Terry." The girl stood up and shook hands with Mark and Jason. "I'm the trainer you'll be working with. Glad you're here." Terry had a warm smile and a friendly way about her.

"Thanks, Terry," Jason said. "It's good to meet you. Have you been a trainer very long?" Jason was surprised. He had been thinking all the trainers were men.

"Three years now. And I've still got so much to learn about these whales. They're wonderful. And smart! You guys will know so much about them by the end of this summer," Terry said. "And you'll really grow to love them, too."

Jason felt excited. He wanted to start learning it all—now! And he wanted to see the whales. Where were they?

"What were you doing with those bottles, Terry?" Mark asked.

Terry closed the top of the box of bottles. "I've been testing to see how much salt is in the water. And I make sure the water temperature stays the same. We don't want the whales to get sick," Terry said. "Oh, here come our other new people."

A pretty girl with short dark hair came over to them. There was a tall boy with her. Mark smiled at the girl. This will keep Mark happy, Jason thought.

"You must be Lyn and Jeff," Terry said. "I'm Terry. These handsome men are Mark and Jason. Welcome!"

"Hi, Terry, Mark, Jason. Sorry we're late," Lyn and Jeff said.

"No problem. We're just about to start now," Terry said. "The other trainer will be here soon. His name is Pat. He's a great guy. Fun to work with. So, let's go over here and talk."

They all sat down beside the whale pool.

"OK, now about your jobs. When you first get here, fill the trainers' buckets with fish. The buckets are in the Cut Shack over there." Terry pointed to a small white building. "I'll take you over there later and show you where everything is."

"What time is the first show?" Jason asked.

"Ten a.m. People start coming in at 9:30. Keep them away from the pool. Tell people in the front rows they'll get wet. Our whales make such big splashes," Terry said. "People are always amazed."

"How do we help the trainers in the show?" Jeff asked.

"You keep people in their seats. And then you help with the whale kiss." Terry smiled at the group.

"The whale kiss?" Mark asked.

"That's when someone gets a kiss from a whale. The trainer picks out a person in the crowd. You go and bring the person down here," Terry said.

"Then what?" Lyn asked.

"You show the person where to stand beside the pool. We give the whale a signal. He jumps up and gives the person a big wet kiss on the cheek. And you give the person a towel to dry off with," Terry said.

"Isn't a kiss kind of dangerous? Aren't these called killer whales?" Jeff asked.

"They are killers only in the wild. And they kill only when they're hungry. At Sea Center our whales are well fed," Terry said.

"Has a killer whale ever attacked a person?" Jason asked.

"There is no record of a killer whale ever attacking a person," Terry said. "But there is always a first time. And we must never forget that."

CHAPTER 4

Meet the Whales

"In a few minutes you'll get to meet Kita and Toshu," Terry said. "But first I want to tell you some things about them. Kita is twenty years old. He's been here sixteen years. Toshu is eighteen, and he's been here at Sea Center thirteen years."

"Where were they captured?" Mark asked.

"Kita was captured near Iceland. Toshu came from near British Columbia," Terry said. "Killer whales like cold oceans."

"I hear killer whales swim in packs. Is that true?" Jason asked.

"Yes. They hunt for food in packs. They're sometimes called the 'wolves of the sea.' That's the smart way to hunt. And killer whales are very smart. Their brains are very large."

"What do they hunt?" Lyn asked.

"Fish, seals, penguins, and even other whales," Terry said. "They hunt walruses and sea otters, too. Grown killer whales can eat two hundred and fifty pounds of food a day."

"Whew! That's one healthy appetite!" Jason said.

"Are killer whales really dolphins?" Lyn asked.

"Yes. They are the biggest, fastest members of the dolphin family," Terry said.

"How much do they weigh?" Jason asked.

"A full-grown male can weigh almost 20,000 pounds. He can be as long as 30 feet, too," said Terry.

"I hope I don't meet one when I'm surfing," Jeff laughed.

"Killer whales will come right up to humans. They seem to want to be petted. This makes them easy to train," Terry said. "They will rub their bodies up against a trainer in the pool."

"How do you start training whales to do tricks?" Jason asked.

"Well, each trainer first spends a long time just watching the whale. You can learn a lot about a whale this way," Terry said.

"What kinds of things?" Mark asked.

"Some whales like to be alone a lot. Others like company. And killer whales have their moods just like people." Terry smiled and stood up. "One day they'll give a great show for us. The next day they might not seem to want to perform at all."

"Will you tell us more about training the whales?" Jeff asked.

"Tomorrow. Right now I want you to meet Kita and Toshu. Come on." Terry started walking over to a high fence. It was behind the big pool. Everybody followed her. She pointed down into the water.

"Do you see the gate down there? We lift that up when the whales go into the show pool. They go back into their home pool after the show," Terry said.

She opened a door in the fence. "Here is where Kita and Toshu live."

Behind the fence was another large pool. But this one wasn't empty. Two big black and white killer whales swam slowly around in it.

Jason couldn't believe it. He was only ten feet away from two killer whales! They were beautiful. Their backs and flippers were very black. Their bodies were white underneath. They looked big, strong, and fast. What power machines, Jason thought.

"Hi, you guys!" Terry sat down by the side of the pool. The whales raced over to her. "Want to meet some new people?"

The whales lifted their heads out of the water at once.

"No fish now. It's almost showtime. But you can have your tongues rubbed," Terry said.

She touched the whales' mouths. Then each whale stuck his tongue out. She began to softly rub their tongues.

"I can't believe it," Lyn said. "Aren't you afraid? Look at all those teeth!"

"About fifty of them. Each one is three inches long and an inch thick," Terry said.

"Awesome!" Jeff whistled.

"Don't worry. We know Kita and Toshu very well. And we've done this hundreds of times. Killer whales love having their tongues rubbed. Want to try it?" Terry asked the group.

"Sure!" Jason sat down beside Terry. Slowly he reached his hand out into Kita's mouth. It looked as though Kita had a thousand sharp teeth. Then Jason carefully put his hand on Kita's big pink tongue.

"Look at that. Kita loves it, Jason," Terry said. "You've got the magic touch."

Mark sat down beside Jason and Terry.

"OK if I try it on Toshu?" he asked Terry.

*Then Jason put his hand
on Kita's big pink tongue.*

"Sure. Go ahead. What lucky whales!" Terry said.

"Did you ever think you'd rub a whale's tongue today, Mark?" Jason laughed.

"No way. Hey, check out these teeth," Mark said. "I sure hope Toshu likes the way I rub his tongue!"

CHAPTER 5

Showtime

"It's nine o'clock. Time to fill the fish buckets for the first show. Follow me!" Terry told the group.

Terry led them into a small white building. "This is the Cut Shack. Hold your noses! And don't worry—it didn't take me too long to get used to it."

"Phew! You're right. Pretty fishy in here," Jeff said.

"You're not kidding," Mark laughed as he held his nose.

There were three big sinks along the wall. They were full of fish and ice.

"Each of us trainers has a bucket. See,

here's mine and here's Pat's," Terry said. "You just fill the buckets up with fish like this. Then you weigh the bucket."

"Why do you have to know how much it weighs?" Lyn asked him.

"To keep a record of how much fish the whales eat." Terry was busy putting fish in her bucket. Jason started to help her. The fish were icy cold.

"We'll do Pat's bucket. OK, Mark? Lyn?" Jeff said.

"OK. But let's fill it fast!" Mark laughed. "The faster, the better."

The Cut Shack door swung open.

"Here you all are!" A short, strong-looking young man came in. "I'm Pat, your other fearless trainer. Welcome to Sea Center! Looks like we've got some great help this summer, Terry! Nobody's afraid to get his hands into the fish buckets!"

Jason liked Pat's jolly smile right away. Pat

would be fun to work for. In fact, everyone at Sea Center seemed to be really nice.

The fish buckets were filled. Then it was time to go back to the big whale pool. People would be coming in soon for the first show of the day.

"Remember, be sure to keep people away from the pool," Terry said. "Each of you pick a part of the crowd to watch. We'll show you where to have people stand for the whale kiss."

Pat and Terry showed the group a small stand beside the pool.

"Have the person stand sideways and lean out a little right here," Pat said. "They might be scared. Tell them not to worry. Kita is a soft kisser. He'll just rise up out of the water and barely touch the person's face."

"We'll meet after the show and talk about how it went. Pat and I better go get dressed for the show now. Good luck!" Terry waved as she and Pat left.

"I'll watch the seats at this end of the pool," Mark said.

"I've got these seats covered," Jason pointed to the center seats.

"Lyn and I will do the far end seats," Jeff said.

Jason felt excited. People were filling up seats now. It was time to get to work. The show would soon be starting. He hoped he and Mark would be able to do a good job.

An old man and woman sat down in the front row. They looked happy and excited as they took their seats.

"Excuse me," Jason said. "If you sit here, you'll get really wet. Can I find you a seat higher up? There are some good places a few rows back. Do you want me to see if I can find two for you?"

"Oh, no," the lady smiled. "We love to get wet! We sit down here every time we come!"

"OK, have fun!" Neat people, Jason

thought. I hope everybody else will be as nice.

Suddenly someone screamed. "Katie!"

Something tiny in white was running towards the pool. A child!

CHAPTER 6

Killer Whale Kiss

Jason ran. His heart pounded. Would he get there in time? So many people were in his way.

"Stop! Katie!" the child's mother screamed.

Jason grabbed for the child's tiny arm as she ran by.

"Got her!" he yelled. They were right at the edge of the pool. Jason had caught Katie just in time.

"Thank you. Oh, thank you so much," the woman said to Jason. "She got away from me. I turned around and she was gone."

"That's OK. She's fine," Jason said. "Better watch her closely in here. Our whales don't like to share their pool!" He gave the child back to the frightened mother.

Wow, some first hour on the job! Jason thought. His heart was pounding hard inside his chest. That was a close one.

Jason watched the crowd. The front rows were all full of teenagers. And the old couple. So far so good. People were staying in their seats.

Suddenly the loudspeaker came on. It was showtime!

"Ladies and gentlemen. Welcome to Sea Center's Whale Show. In just a minute you'll meet Kita and Toshu. But, first, two big rules here. Keep your children in their seats. And don't go near the whale pool."

The crowd clapped and cheered. They wanted the show to start.

"Now, meet our trainers, Terry Hall and Pat Woods!" The loudspeaker started up again.

Terry and Pat ran up to the side of the pool

and bowed. They wore white shorts and shirts. People clapped and cheered. Pat picked up a microphone.

"We're ready now to meet the stars of our show. Ladies and gentlemen, Sea Center's own Kita and Toshu!"

Jason saw Terry push a button on the far side of the pool. This opened the underwater gate for the whales.

Suddenly two giant dark shapes shot into the pool.

"And here they come! Kita and Toshu! Thirty-five thousand pounds of killer whale! They're on their speed run now. Look at them go!" Pat said on the loudspeaker. "Thirty miles per hour!"

The whales raced around the tank. Then Kita suddenly jumped high into the air. His body was all shiny in the sunlight. The crowd cheered. Then Kita came down. A high wave of water hit the first rows of seats. People screamed and laughed. They were having a wonderful time getting wet.

Pat threw Kita a fish from his bucket as a reward for the big jump.

"Killer whales can jump their whole body length in the air." Terry was speaking now. "Can you imagine the strength it must take to lift nine tons into the air? These whales make these jumps or 'breaches,' in the wild, too. Not just here in the show."

Terry gave Toshu a signal. She raised her right arm over her head. Toshu began to race around the pool. Then he jumped into the air. Suddenly he was moving backwards up on his tail!

"Toshu's tail walk, ladies and gentlemen! What do you think of that?" Terry asked the crowd. Everyone cheered and clapped excitedly.

Toshu swam over to Terry. He lifted his head out of the water. Terry reached down and petted his head.

Amazing! thought Jason. How do they train the whales to do these tricks? I've got to learn how they do it.

Kita and Toshu did lots more tricks in the show. They jumped over a high net. They did back swan dives together. Jason watched Terry and Pat give the whales hand signals before each trick. Terry started to spin her hands fast in a circle. Then Toshu brought in a beach ball she had thrown him.

Now it was time for the whale kiss. Everybody wanted to be the one Terry picked.

"The pretty teenaged girl in the pink shirt!" Terry called out. "Come down front for your kiss from Kita!"

Mark went up and brought the girl down to the pool. He sure looks happy, Jason thought to himself.

The girl got up on the stand by the side of the pool.

"Just stand sideways like this. Lean out over the water a little," Mark told her.

"I'm a little scared," the girl said.

"Don't worry. Kita is very gentle. See, he's starting to come over now." Mark pointed to Kita's dark shape under the water.

"Kita is coming up for the kiss," Pat said on the loudspeaker. "There he is!"

Kita's huge head came up out of the water. The girl started to step back. Kita's head came up higher and higher. Then he lightly touched her face with his mouth. Kita slipped back down into the pool. The crowd cheered.

"And there it is—a killer whale kiss!" Pat said into the microphone. He was at the girl's side now. "How did that feel?"

"Great! I can't believe it. I got kissed by a killer whale!" the girl said.

"What's your name? Where are you from?" Pat asked the girl.

"I'm Kim Barnes and I'm from right here in

Ocean Park." The crowd cheered and yelled.

"Hey, Mark, have you got that name?" Jason whispered to his brother. Mark smiled. This sure was a new way to meet a girl!

*Then Kita lightly touched
her face with his mouth.*

CHAPTER 7

Learning the Way

The first show was over. The seats were all empty. Pat and Terry sat down with the group beside the whale pool.

"You all did great. And it was quick work you did, Jason, grabbing that little girl. We heard about it backstage," Pat said. "That doesn't happen very often. But we always have to keep an eye on those little ones."

"You all kept the people in their seats. The girl got her kiss. Good job!" Terry told the group. "Next show in two hours."

"Do the whales have to rest up after a show?" Lyn asked. "It seems like they work so hard."

"They'll sometimes rest between shows," Terry said. "They won't move around much. Did you know that when whales sleep, only half their brain sleeps? Whales have to think to breathe. If their whole brain slept, they'd drown."

"Amazing," Jeff said. "Kind of scary to think about."

"For each trick you first give the whales a hand signal. Will you show us some of those signals again?" Jason asked. "I'd like to learn them myself."

"A lot of what the whales do are not tricks. They're things whales do naturally. Like jumping up into the air," Pat said. "And what we call 'sky hopping.' That's when they seem to be standing in the water with their heads up. We just get them to do these things in our show. Now, let's go over those hand signals. Maybe we should first talk about how we start training the whales in the beginning. That is, if you'd like to hear about it."

"Oh, yes," Lyn said. And it was clear the others agreed with her.

"For each new whale we choose a special whistle like this." Terry showed the group a small silver whistle. "We use it for only that whale. It has its own tone." Terry blew softly on the whistle. A high-pitched sound came out.

"We try to feed the new whales by hand. If that isn't possible, we put food into the pool," Pat explained. "Each time the whale takes a piece of food, we blow the whistle. Soon the whale starts to think that food and the whistle go together."

"We trainers watch the whale and blow the whistle whenever he does something naturally that we want him to repeat," Terry said. "The whale will then swim over to us for a food reward."

"How do you teach them to jump so high out of the water?" Jason asked.

"Well, they do jump naturally, but we train them to jump even higher here," Pat answered. "We use a long pole to gently touch the top of the whale's head. We blow the whistle at the same time, and give him a fish. We do this lots of times."

"The whale soon begins to touch the pole by himself when we hold it at water level," Terry said. "Then we always give him a fish. Next, we start slowly raising the pole higher above the water. The whale jumps up to touch the pole and get his fish reward. In a short while, the whales are jumping twenty feet out of the water!"

"I can't believe how fast they learn things," Lyn said.

"Remember, all of the things the whales do, like jumping, are really natural actions for them. Being in a show doesn't hurt them at all. They seem to really like performing," Terry told the group.

"Are there some tricks a whale refuses to do?" Jeff asked.

"Oh, yes, and they let you know about it," Pat laughed. "We tried to get Kita to let us ride on his back around the pool. He would let us ride to the center of the pool and then leave us there! We ended up dropping that trick from the show."

Pat and Terry next showed the group all the hand signals for the show. Jason couldn't wait to get home and write them down. But first there were three more shows to do! And fish buckets to fill for the trainers.

The next shows went by fast. People stayed in their seats. No babies ran for the water. There was so much to learn from Pat and Terry! And so much to learn about Kita and Toshu!

Sea Center closed at six. Jason and Mark walked out with Lyn and Jeff after they had all changed clothes.

"Pretty good first day," Jason said. "No sitting around on this job. Pat and Terry sure kept us busy!"

"Boy, those whales can sure throw water!" Jeff laughed. "Couldn't believe how soaked I got!"

"Felt kind of good. That sun was hot!" Mark said. "Did you guys have any trouble on your side of the show?"

"No. People were pretty good," Lyn said. "Nobody wanted to take a swim with the killer whales."

"Well, see you tomorrow morning." Mark and Jason waved good-bye and started for the bus stop.

"That shower sure felt good," Mark said. "Hope we got all the fish smell off. They might throw us off the bus!"

"We smell great! Hey, what about the whale kiss girl? Get her phone number?" Jason asked with a grin.

45

"Of course! This job may turn out to be OK. First day sure was! Hey, high five!" The boys clapped hands in the air. Then they ran for the bus.

CHAPTER 8

A Talk with Terry

Mark and Jason went to the Cut Shack first the next morning. It was their day to fill the fish buckets. Lyn and Jeff would do it the next day.

"Hey, Mark, let's get to be trainers. Then we won't have to fill these buckets any more," Jason said. "We'll just come in here and pick them up."

"I bet it takes a long time to get to be a trainer. There's a lot to learn. And you can't make mistakes in a show. Not with two killer whales," Mark said. "Hey, these buckets are full. We're out of here!"

The boys walked over to the back pool.

Kita and Toshu swam slowly around in the water. Kita raised his head and looked at the boys.

"Do you think he knows us? Hey, Kita!" Mark and Jason went to the side of the pool. Kita swam over. Then Toshu came, too. The boys put out their hands and rubbed the top of both whales' heads.

"This is great! They love it," Jason said. "Their skin feels just like a peeled hardboiled egg, doesn't it? I sure hope we'll get to try working with these guys this summer. I really want to try out those hand signals."

"I think our hands will be busy in fish buckets this summer," Mark laughed.

Just then Terry came over to the boys.

"You guys are going to spoil these whales," she laughed. "But they sure love to be touched, don't they?" Terry knelt down to rub the top of Toshu's head. "Did I ever show you where a whale's ears are?" She pointed to two small holes behind Toshu's eyes.

"They're sure hard to see," Jason said.

"Yes. And no one knows exactly how whales hear. Around the inside parts of a whale's ear are hollow spaces with a sort of padding in them. These protect the ears from pressure when the whale dives," Terry told the boys.

"Do whales hear sounds under water?" Mark asked.

"Yes. And they depend a lot on sound because there's not much light under water. Six hundred feet down, it's almost completely dark!" Terry said. "So whales use sound to 'see' their way around."

"How do they do this?" Mark asked.

"They make sounds and then listen to them come back. This way they can tell what something is under water. And they can also tell how big and how far away it is." Terry gently touched one of Toshu's small ears.

"What kinds of sounds would a whale make under water?" Jason asked.

"They're a type of click. They sound a little like a creaking door," Terry said. "The whale makes the clicks somewhere inside its nose. The sounds pass through his forehead, then they go out into the water in the direction the whale wants them to go."

"I've heard Kita and Toshu make lots of sounds in the pool," Mark said. "They're like squeaks. Even barks and grunts."

"And whistles. We think they use these sounds to tell other whales where they are and even what mood they're in. And they sometimes slap their tails down in the water to show they're mad about something. That can mean a big splash. Kita's tail is nine feet from end to end!" Terry said.

"Nine feet!" Jason whistled.

"They snap their jaws together when they're upset, too. You love to do that, don't you,

Toshu?" Terry slowly stroked the huge whale's head.

"A whale's eyes are really small for an animal so large, aren't they?" Mark asked.

"Yes. And look how far back on his head they are, too," Terry said. "A whale can only see out to the side with each eye. He can't look straight in front of himself."

"Is that why killer whales lift their heads straight up out of the water—so they can see what is happening on the surface?" Jason asked.

"Right. That's how they look around them," Terry answered.

"How long could a killer whale stay under water without coming up for air?" Mark asked Terry.

"Usually their dive is for less than a minute. But some killer whales have been known to stay under for five minutes or more. When the whale comes up, he lets old air out through the blowhole. When he breathes, he brings fresh air into the blowhole. The hole closes over when he's under water." Terry pointed to the small hole in the top of Toshu's head.

"Hey, Jason, we'd better get over to the main pool. It's almost showtime!" Mark stood up quickly. "I forgot to look at my watch. It was so great hearing all that about the whales, Terry. Pretty amazing creatures!"

"They sure are, Mark. I got so busy talking I forgot the time, too. You both seem to have a special feeling about whales. And that makes me feel good. See you poolside!"

"Well, see you later, guys." Terry smiled and waved as she hurried off.

"Well, see you later, guys," Jason said to Toshu and Kita. "Give 'em some big splashes today!"

The boys hurried out to the big pool. Lyn and Jeff were helping people find seats. Mark and Jason got busy, too. Today was Saturday and the crowd was bigger.

"Be extra careful on the crowded days. That's when accidents happen. People do things you don't see." Jason remembered when Terry said this. Today would be one of those days. He knew he was going to have to watch the crowd extra carefully.

CHAPTER 9

The Signal

The loudspeaker came on. It was time for the show to start. Mark and Jason felt excited. It was great to be a part of this.

Kita and Toshu put on a perfect show. The crowd loved them. Every jump was beautiful. It was true—the whales seemed to love to perform for the crowd.

"Kita and Toshu are in a wonderful mood today," Pat told the crowd. "Must be they like Saturdays."

Or maybe it was because we scratched their heads this morning. Jason smiled.

Each show lasted a long time. Kita and Toshu did some extra jumps and speed runs.

Now it was taking a long time for the crowd to leave.

A lot of people wanted to look at Kita. He was still in the big tank. Toshu was in the back pool now. More than once Mark and Jason had to warn people not to go so close to the edge of the pool.

Suddenly there was a scream! And a splash. Someone had fallen into the pool. Where? Jason couldn't see. There were too many people. He pushed through the crowd.

"He can't swim! Someone help him!" a voice yelled. More people started screaming.

Jason rushed to the edge of the pool. There he saw the body of a small boy going under water. The boy was far from the side of the pool. Jason got set to dive. Then he saw Kita. The whale was swimming towards the boy. Jason stared. What was Kita going to do? People were screaming. And the trainers had left the pool.

Then Jason knew. Kita could save the boy. The whale was trained to bring anything in that fell into the pool. But he needs the signal. Spin your hands fast. You bring in the beach

Jason rushed to the edge of the pool.

ball, Kita. Now bring in this child.

Jason gave the signal. He spun his hands. Kita raced towards the child's sinking body. Then he stopped. He softly dipped his head under water. He pushed the child's body up. Then he began to push the child towards the side of the pool.

By this time Mark had reached Jason's side.

"Let's go," Mark said. And the boys dove in and met Kita. Together they brought the child in with the whale.

Pat was there to reach down for the child. "I've got him now. Great work, guys." He pulled the little boy from the water.

Mark and Jason saw the paramedics bending over the child. Please be OK, they whispered. Be alive.

The boys hung onto the side of the pool. And Kita rested his head against their backs.

"He's OK! He's breathing. We're taking

him out," someone yelled. The crowd cheered. The child's mother rushed over to Mark and Jason.

"Thank you. Thank you so much," she cried. Then she was gone.

Pat and Jeff bent down to the boys.

"Are you OK? Take our hands. We're pulling you out," they said.

"OK. Let me do this first," Jason told them. He softly rubbed the top of Kita's head. Then he gave his hand to Pat. Jeff pulled Mark up. Lyn and Terry wrapped big towels around the boys.

"You and Kita make quite a team!" Pat said. "You don't need us out here. That was great work you did. Quick thinking."

"Thanks, Pat." Mark and Jason turned to look down at Kita. The whale was still there by the side of the pool.

"Kita's an amazing animal. He sure knew what to do," Jason said.

"You gave him the signal," Terry said. "You learn fast. Maybe you could try out more signals with the whales this summer. You interested?"

"Yes! Wow, I'd love that." Jason couldn't believe it. It was really happening. He'd get to work with the whales! He had been hoping for that all along.

"Let's get you guys to the showers," Pat said. "Out of those wet clothes."

"Wait. There's one thing I want to do," Mark said. "Any fish left in that bucket over there?"

"One or two," Terry said. "Why?"

Mark ran over and picked up the fish. Then he threw them to Kita.

"Hey, is this the guy who didn't want to fill fish buckets?" Jason laughed.

"Same guy. OK, let's hit the showers!" Mark said. "I've got a date tonight."

"With the girl that Kita kissed?" Jason asked.

"That's the one! High five, Jason. We're outa here!" The boys slapped hands in the air. They waved to everyone at the pool. Then they ran for the showers.